# PIXIE TRICKS

## DOUBLE TROUBLE DWARFS

◆

Catch all of the
# PIXIE TRICKS
adventures!

# PIXIE TRICKS

## DOUBLE TROUBLE DWARFS

◆

### BY TRACEY WEST

**SCHOLASTIC INC.**
New York  Toronto  London  Auckland  Sydney
Mexico City  New Delhi  Hong Kong  Buenos Aires

ISBN 0-439-17983-1

Copyright © 2000 by Tracey West

Interior and sticker illustrations by Thea Kliros

All rights reserved. Published by Scholastic Inc. SCHOLASTIC and associated logos are trademarks and/or registered trademarks of Scholastic Inc.

24 23 22 21 20 19 18 17 16 15 14 13          6 7 8 9/0

Printed in the U.S.A.          40
First Scholastic printing, March 2001

In memory of Tisha, the best dog ever and my best friend for ten years. For Elvira, a cranky cat with a soft heart; and for Ginger and Irvin, my two new doggy buddies. Thanks for keeping me company all day!

— T. W.

# ·:· CONTENTS ·:·

Fourteen pixies have escaped;

They're causing so much trouble.

Sprite and Violet's secret job

Is to trick them on the double!

So far they've tricked Jolt and Fixit,

And the sprite Aquamarina, too.

Buttercup and Bogey Bill

Were another tricky two.

They've tricked Ragamuffin and Sport,

And also Rusella and Pix.

Will they catch the last five pixies?

Keep reading *Pixie Tricks*!

## Chapter One
## Five More to Go

"Beastie Bites is the best cereal in the whole world!" Sprite said.

The tiny fairy crunched a piece of the bright green cereal. He flapped his wings happily.

Sometimes Violet Briggs still couldn't believe she had a fairy for a friend. But she did.

She met Sprite weeks ago. He came through a magic door in the oak tree in Violet's backyard. He asked for Violet's help.

Sprite told her that fourteen fairies had escaped from his world. The Otherworld. The pixies were going to cause big trouble in the human world, and he needed Violet's help to send them back home.

Violet agreed to help. To send the fairies back, they had to trick them. They had tricked nine pixies so far.

Now they were sitting under the oak tree, eating breakfast. Violet wanted to plan their next move.

"Everything always seems to happen by surprise," Violet said. "I think we should make a list. We should go over the last five pixies one by one."

"Sounds fine to me," Sprite said. His green eyes twinkled. "Of course, I can't promise there won't be any surprises. That's just how it goes with fairies sometimes."

"We'll see," Violet said. She turned the pages of the *Book of Tricks*. Sprite's tiny book told how to trick all of the escaped pixies.

"We're still looking for Hinky Pink," Violet said. She wrote his name on a piece of paper. "Hinky Pink changes the weather."

"Then there's Spoiler," Sprite said. "She's always messing things up."

Violet wrote down Spoiler's name.

"We can't forget Finn," Violet said. "The wizard who led the escape."

Sprite shuddered at the sound of the wizard's name.

"That's three," Violet said. "There should be two more pixies on the loose."

Sprite finished his last bite of cereal. He flew onto Violet's shoulder.

"I'm not sure who they could be," he said.

Violet flipped through the book. She stopped on a page with a rhyme on it.

"Who are Greenie and Meanie?" she asked.

"I know those two!" Sprite said. "Greenie and Meanie are dwarfs. They are twins, too."

"The escaped pixies all like to cause trouble. What do you think these two might be up to?" Violet asked.

Sprite thought. "In the Otherworld, they were always trying to make money. But not in an honest way."

"You mean they stole things?" Violet asked.

"I'm not sure," Sprite said. His cheeks blushed dark green. "You know I don't have the best memory."

"That's okay," Violet said. She wrote Greenie and Meanie's names on her paper. "It's enough to start with."

Just then, Violet saw her friend Brittany run into the yard. Sprite quickly hid in Violet's pocket.

"Violet, it's terrible!" Brittany said. "Buster is missing!"

## Chapter Two
# Danger in the Dog Park

"Buster? Your dog?" Violet asked.

Brittany nodded. She blinked back tears.

"He disappeared in the dog park yesterday," Brittany said. She handed Violet a piece of paper. It was a picture of a beagle.

"Brittany, I'm so sorry!" Violet said.

A car horn beeped.

"That's my dad," Brittany said. "I've got to go look for Buster. Let me know if you see him, okay?"

# MISSING

Buster. He's brown and white and very friendly.

If you find him, please call 555-3675.

Violet nodded. "Okay. Don't worry, Brittany. We'll find him!"

Brittany ran out of the yard. Sprite flew out of Violet's pocket.

"Poor Brittany!" Sprite said. "I have a pet caterpillar back in the Otherworld. I'd hate it if anything bad happened to Squeaky."

"Pet caterpillar?" Violet asked with surprise. "Never mind. We've got to help Brittany."

"What about tricking pixies?" Sprite asked.

"We can do that later," Violet said. "With your pixie dust, we can look in a lot of places. I bet we'll find Buster fast."

"You're right," Sprite said. He reached into the small bag that hung around his waist.

Sprite pulled out a handful of sparkling dust. One sprinkle of pixie dust could take them anywhere they wanted to go.

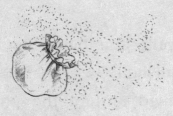

"Where should we look?" Sprite asked.

"Let's start with the dog park," Violet said.

Sprite threw the pixie dust over them. "To the dog park!" he said.

Violet held her nose. Pixie dust always made her sneeze.

Violet's skin tingled. The backyard disappeared. In a flash, they were in a green, grassy park.

Violet had come to the dog park with Brittany before. People brought their dogs here to run around and play.

"You'd better hide in my pocket again," Violet told Sprite. "Somebody might see you."

"Okay," Sprite grumbled. "But my wings always get squished."

Violet walked around the park. Fluffy

little dogs yapped at each other. Big shaggy dogs chased balls and Frisbees. Their owners talked, enjoying the sunny day.

"It looks pretty normal here," Violet said. Then she stopped. "Hey — what's that?"

Trees bordered the park. Violet walked over to the trees. There were signs on each one.

"Missing: Poochie," Violet read. "Missing: Rex. Missing: Goldie."

Sprite's head popped up. He looked at the signs.

"Look at all these missing dogs!" he said.

"There's something strange about this," Violet said. "One missing dog is normal. But lots of missing dogs sounds like pixie trouble to me."

Sprite sniffed the air. "You may be right," he said. "I smell pixie dust!"

"You do?" Violet asked.

"I'm a Royal Pixie Tricker, remember?" Sprite said. "We learned how to sniff out pixie dust in school. It's coming from over there!" Sprite pointed to a bunch of trees.

"Then let's go!" Violet said.

Violet tried to walk through the trees without making a sound. But sometimes she stepped on a twig or crackly leaf. Sprite sniffed and sniffed. He told her which way to go.

Then Violet heard a voice.

"What a pretty pup you are!"

Violet ducked behind a tree. Then she and Sprite slowly peeked out and looked.

Two dwarfs stood nearby. One of them held a small dog in its arms.

"It's Greenie and Meanie!" Sprite whispered to Violet.

# Chapter Three
## Spoiled!

Violet froze. She studied the dwarfs. They were both almost as tall as she was. They looked a lot alike. But one had a short black beard and beady eyes. He had a mean look on his face.

"That's Meanie," Sprite whispered.

The other dwarf was Greenie. He had a friendly, round face. He wore a long green cap. He stroked the little dog in his lap. But the tiny puppy shivered nervously.

"It looks like they're stealing that dog!" Violet said.

"Oh, dear," Sprite said. "What should we do?"

"Let's look in the *Book of Tricks*," Violet said. "Maybe we can trick them right here."

Sprite took the book out of his bag.

"Not so fast!" a voice called out.

A shower of pixie dust sprinkled the book. Then the book flew out of Sprite's hands.

"Spoiler!" Violet cried. "Stop it right now."

A small pixie popped out from behind a tree. Spoiler had two ponytails on top of her head. She wore overalls and a yellow-striped shirt.

Spoiler laughed. "I don't want to stop! I have too much fun spoiling things for you."

Sprite looked at Spoiler sadly. "Why are you doing this? We used to be friends back in the Otherworld."

Violet couldn't believe it. "Friends? You two?" Spoiler had caused them so much trouble. She couldn't imagine what kind of friend would do that.

Spoiler frowned. "We were friends until Queen Mab made you a Royal Pixie Tricker. I would have made a great Pixie Tricker!"

"I had no idea you wanted to be a Pixie Tricker," Sprite said.

"Finn knows how talented I am," Spoiler said. "When he takes over the human world, I'll be his right-hand pixie."

"I can talk to Queen Mab for you," Sprite said. "I'm sure there's room for one more student in Royal Pixie Tricker school."

Spoiler stuck out her tongue. Then she threw some pixie dust and disappeared.

Violet spotted the *Book of Tricks* in the grass.

"I've got the book!" she said. "We can trick Greenie and Meanie now!"

"No we can't," Sprite said, shaking his head. "They're gone."

Violet looked. The dwarfs and the stolen dog were nowhere in sight.

"They must have heard us," Violet said. She opened the book. "It doesn't matter.

We'll find out how to trick them. And we'll save all those poor dogs!"

Violet flipped through the *Book of Tricks*. Then she found Greenie and Meanie's rhyme. She read it aloud.

"'Greenie and Meanie love all dogs,
They train them in a special way.
But to trick these dwarf brothers,
You must get them both to obey!'"

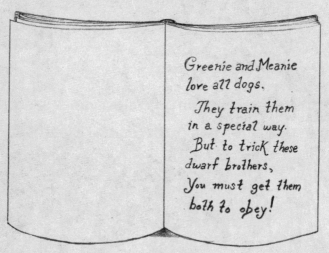

Greenie and Meanie love all dogs.

They train them in a special way.

But to trick these dwarf brothers,

You must get them both to obey!

## Chapter Four
# Where Are They?

"Did you read that right?" Sprite asked.

"I think so," Violet said. She squinted at the tiny type. "It says we have to get them both to obey."

Sprite fluttered in front of Violet's face. "That won't be easy," he said. "Dwarfs can be very stubborn."

Violet looked at her watch. "It's getting close to lunchtime," she said. "Aunt Anne will be looking for me. We can figure this out at home."

"Right!" Sprite said. He sprinkled them with pixie dust, and they were in the back-yard in a flash.

Violet's cousin Leon was waiting for them. He stood in front of the oak tree with his arms folded in front of him.

"Were you pixie tricking without me?" Leon asked. He hated to be left out of anything.

Leon and his mom, Violet's Aunt Anne, lived in the same house with Violet and her parents. Leon was the only other person who knew about Sprite and the pixie secret. Violet was always afraid that Leon would mess things up. But she had to admit that he had helped them a number of times.

"We weren't exactly pixie tricking," Violet

told her cousin. She explained how they had gone out to find Brittany's dog. Instead, they had found Greenie and Meanie.

"They're stealing dogs?" Leon cried. "Let's get them! How do we trick them, anyway?"

"The *Book of Tricks* says that we're supposed to make them obey us," said Violet.

"No problem," Leon said. "I'm sure those dwarfs won't want to mess with a guy like me. I'll bet they'll do anything I say."

Sprite flew up to Leon.

"I wouldn't be so sure about that," Sprite said. "Meanie is pretty tough!"

"I'm not scared," Leon said. "I can take on any pixie!"

Violet sighed. Her cousin always tried to act brave. But she knew Sprite was right. Meanie was tough. And his name sounded, well, mean!

They had to come up with a plan to trick Meanie and Greenie. And it'd better be a good one!

# Chapter Five
## A Plan

During lunch, Violet, Sprite, and Leon talked about what to do.

"I have an idea," Leon said. He bit into his sandwich. "We could use a dog as bait. The dwarfs would take the dog. Then we could follow them to their hiding place."

Violet frowned. Leon's plan wasn't bad. But it made her nervous. "That could be very dangerous for the dog. Besides, we don't have one."

Leon turned to Sprite. "Couldn't you make one out of magic?"

"Goodness, no," Sprite said. "I couldn't make something like a dog out of thin air." He paused. "Of course, I could always . . ."

"What?" Leon asked.

"Well, I could turn *you* into a dog," Sprite said. "Just for a little while."

Leon shook his head. "Oh, no! I saw how Aquamarina turned those people into fish. That was creepy. And they almost stayed that way forever."

Violet tried not to smile. Aquamarina was a water sprite they had tricked. She had turned Leon into a fish-boy. Leon didn't remember it. Violet and Sprite decided that was a good thing.

"Come on, Leon," Violet said. "Just think.

You could be a hero and save all those dogs."

"Then why don't *you* do it?"

Sprite looked at Violet. He had a nervous look in his eye. She understood his concern. She would let Sprite turn her into a dog if she really had to. But she couldn't figure things out if she was a dog. And she was better at solving different kinds of problems than Leon.

She had to convince Leon to do it.

Violet took a deep breath. "Because you're so brave, Leon," she said. "Remember how you bopped Bogey Bill over the head? And how you tricked Jolt in the video game?"

Leon looked suspicious. "I thought you said I tricked those pixies by mistake."

"Of course not!" Violet said. She hated

lying to Leon. But it was for the dogs, after all. "You saved the day. You can save the day again if Sprite turns you into a dog. You'd make a much better dog than I would."

Leon swallowed the last bite of sandwich.

"Maybe," he said. He turned to Sprite. "Can I be something cool and tough? Like a German shepherd? Or a pit bull?"

"Anything you want!" Sprite said.

"All right!" Leon stood up. "I can see it's all up to me now. I will save the day, as usual."

Violet cringed. Leon could act like such a big shot sometimes! This wasn't going to be easy.

"So what do I do?" Leon asked.

Sprite flipped through the *Book of Tricks*. "Logs . . . fogs . . . pollywogs . . . ah, here it is! Dogs!"

"This should be easy," Sprite said with a smile.

Sprite flew on top of Leon's head. He sprinkled pixie dust over him. Leon watched the pixie dust fall.

Violet wondered what would happen. Sprite's magic didn't always work.

Sprite said a little rhyme.

> *"Wagging tail,*
> *chasing mail,*
> *man's best friend,*
> *from end to end!"*

"What is that supposed to do?" Leon asked. "Are you sure you used the right spell, Sprite? I don't feel anything. This isn't going to — *yip!*"

Violet watched in amazement as fur

started to cover Leon's body. His arms and feet turned into tiny paws. A fluffy tail sprang up behind him. Then his ears started to grow. They grew longer and longer.

Leon was really turning into a dog!

## Chapter Six
# Leon the Poodle

Soon Leon the boy was gone. In his place was Leon the fluffy white poodle.

"What are you two looking at?" Leon asked. "Am I a big, tough dog? Did it work?"

Violet and Sprite couldn't speak. It was too weird hearing Leon's voice come from a dog.

"It worked splendidly," Sprite finally said.

Sprite looked at Violet and shrugged. Violet had seen that look before. It meant, "Sorry! I'm new at this, remember?"

"Do I look tough?" Leon asked. He wagged his poofy tail.

Violet thought he was the cutest little dog she had ever seen. But she couldn't tell that to Leon.

"You look real mean," she said. "If I didn't know it was you, I would run away."

Pleased, Leon licked his pretty white fur.

"We must hurry," Sprite said. "This spell won't last long."

Violet picked up Leon. Sprite threw pixie dust over them. In a flash they were back in the dog park.

"How do we get the dwarfs to steal me?" Leon asked.

"*Shhhh,* Leon," Violet said. "We can't let anyone hear you."

Leon whimpered and rested his chin on his paws.

"I think we should make a big fuss over you," Violet said.

"That's right!" Sprite said. "We'll make it so those dwarfs can't resist you."

Sprite climbed into Violet's pocket. Violet walked Leon to the edge of the dog park, by the trees. No one else was around.

"Aren't you the most beautiful dog in the world?" Violet said in a loud voice. "You're so talented!"

Leon got the hint. He sat down. He rolled over. He played dead.

So far, there was no sign of the dwarfs.

"Come on, you can do better than that, Leon," Violet whispered.

Leon growled a little. Then he walked on his two hind legs. He did a back flip.

"Wonderful!" Violet said. "You're the best doggie ever!"

"Yip, yip, yip!" barked Leon.

"I think it's time," Sprite whispered.

Violet nodded. She patted Leon on the head.

"You stay right here, doggie," Violet said loudly. "I'm going to get you a treat. I'll be right back."

Violet walked away. She hid behind a tree.

"I wonder if the dwarfs will take the bait," Sprite whispered.

They did not have to wait long to find out.

Greenie and Meanie came out of the woods. The two dwarfs snuck up on Leon.

Leon turned his head. He started to run!

"Leon's not supposed to do that," Sprite said. "He's supposed to let the dwarfs catch him."

"That's Leon for you," Violet said.

Greenie took a silver dog leash off of his belt. He threw the leash like a lasso.

*"Yip, yip, yip!"* cried Leon the dog.

The leash landed around Leon's neck. Greenie pulled Leon toward him. He picked up Leon. Then the two dwarfs darted into the trees.

"Let's go!" Sprite said. "It's our only chance!"

Violet ran after the dwarfs. Sprite flew alongside her.

"I can't see them," Violet said.

*"Yip, yip, yip!"*

They followed the sound of Leon's voice.

"How smart of Leon," Sprite said.

Violet thought Leon was probably just yipping because he was nervous. It didn't matter. They followed Leon's yipping to a clearing shaped like a circle.

Violet gasped.

In the middle of the clearing was a large pen. And the pen was filled with dogs!

# Chapter Seven
## Caught!

"They've trapped the dogs," Sprite said.

The pen was made of sticks and twigs tied together with vines. The top of the pen was open. But the walls were too high for the dogs to jump over.

Dogs of all colors and sizes were trapped inside. Violet saw Brittany's dog, Buster. She saw Leon the poodle, too.

Meanie sat on a tree stump. He punched

numbers into a calculator. Greenie fed treats to the dogs through the holes in the pen.

Meanie looked at Greenie. He frowned crossly. "Don't go wasting all those treats," he said. "They cost a lot of money, you know."

Greenie put the treats back in his pocket. "Whatever you say, Meanie," he said. But Violet saw that he still had a treat in his hand. He gave the treat to a small brown dog while Meanie wasn't looking.

"What now?" Sprite asked Violet.

"The book says we have to make the dwarfs obey," Violet said. "We might as well give it a try."

Violet took a brave step into the clearing. Sprite flew next to her. He held out his Royal Pixie Tricker medal.

"In the name of Queen Mab," Sprite said in his loudest voice, "we order you to go back to the Otherworld!"

Greenie fell to his knees. "P-p-p-please don't hurt us," Greenie said. "Don't hurt the nice doggies."

"Of course we won't hurt you," Violet said. She felt sorry for the dwarf. He looked so scared. "We just want you to stop causing trouble."

Meanie raised an eyebrow. "So you want
us to go back to the Otherworld?" he asked.

Violet and Sprite nodded.

"No problem!" he said. "We just need a
few more days. And we're taking these dogs
with us!"

"Oh, dear!" Sprite said. "You can't do
that!"

Meanie stood up. He put his hands on his hips. "Says who?"

"Says Queen Mab," Sprite said. "I mean —"

"Those dogs belong to people," Violet said. "You can't take them away. Their owners will miss them."

"What do I care?" Meanie asked. "There

are plenty of dogs in the human world. They can always get more."

"It's not the same," Violet said. "You don't understand."

Sprite held out the medal again. "I'm afraid we'll have to stop you!" he said.

"That's what you think!" Meanie said. "Greenie, take care of them!"

Greenie looked at his brother. "But they seem nice," he said.

"Do you want them to take away your doggies?" Meanie asked.

Greenie sniffled. "No, Meanie."

Many dog leashes were hanging from the pen. Greenie reached for one of them.

"Let's get out of here!" Violet cried.

Violet and Sprite tried to get away. But Greenie moved quickly. He threw leashes around Violet's hands and feet. He threw a small leash around Sprite's hands and wings.

They were caught! They couldn't move an inch.

"Sorry," Greenie said. "I can't let you take away my doggies!"

## Chapter Eight
# Doggie Tricks

Violet tried to break free. She couldn't. She slumped down on the ground.

Sprite didn't have any luck, either. He leaned back on Violet's leg.

"What now?" Sprite asked her.

"Can we use magic to escape?" Violet asked.

"I don't think so," Sprite said. "These aren't magic knots. These are real knots. I'm

not sure how to undo them. And I can't get to my pixie dust."

"Well, maybe we could try talking to Greenie and Meanie," Violet suggested. "Maybe we can talk them into letting us go."

"*Yip, yip, yip!*" Leon said. He poked his head outside the pen. He didn't look happy.

Violet gave him a look that said, "Don't worry." Then she looked at Greenie. He seemed a little nicer than his brother.

"So you really like these dogs," Violet said.

Greenie nodded. "They're so fluffy and warm and cuddly. They're my friends."

"Why do you want so many?" she asked.

"That's Meanie's idea," Greenie said. "We're going to take them back to the Otherworld. We're going to start a zoo."

"A doggie zoo?" Violet asked.

Meanie jumped up. "We're going to make

a fortune! Fairies will come from all over the Otherworld to see our amazing dogs."

"They look like ordinary dogs to me," Violet said. "Why would fairies pay to see them?"

"There are no dogs in the Otherworld," Sprite said. "Only birds and bugs and butter-flies and things."

Greenie nodded again. "And our doggies are special."

"What do you mean?" Violet asked.

Greenie took some pixie dust out of his pocket. He blew it on the shaggy brown dog in the pen.

The dog magically appeared outside the pen. Greenie picked up three small balls on the ground.

"Show them what you can do, Sparky!" Greenie said. He threw the balls in the air.

Sparky stood up on his hind legs. He grabbed the balls in his paws. He threw them in the air and juggled them.

"Wow!" Violet had to admit she had never seen a dog do that before.

Greenie threw some more pixie dust. "Now you, Buster!" Greenie said.

Brittany's dog appeared outside the pen.

Sparky jumped on Buster's back and did a handstand. Buster ran in circles, and Sparky kept his balance perfectly.

Greenie clapped his hands. "Good doggies!" he said. Sparky jumped up and licked his face.

"That was amazing," Violet told Greenie. "I can see how much you love these dogs. But their owners love them, too. Just think how much they must miss them."

"Stop meddling!" Meanie said crossly. He looked up at the sun. "That retriever we've had our eye on should be taking its walk about now. Let's go get it, Greenie."

"You mean you're not going to let us go?" Sprite asked.

Meanie laughed. "I'll let you go. When we're back in the Otherworld with these dogs!"

Greenie sent Sparky and Buster back to the pen. He grabbed a dog leash. Then he and Meanie walked into the woods.

Leon spoke up. "Nice work, guys. Those dwarfs really look like they're ready to obey you."

"Very funny, Leon," Violet said.

"It's not funny," said her cousin. "If you don't think of something soon, I'm going to be stuck in an Otherworld zoo!"

**Queen Mab**

**Robert B. Gnome**

**Greenie and Meanie— Sparky and Beastie Bites**

**Ragamuffin— A Matching Outfit**

**Spoiler's Books**

**Rusella— Alphabet Soup**

ISBN 0-439-26084-1 Copyright © 2001 by Scholastic Inc. Published by Scholastic Inc., 555 Broadway, New York, NY 10012-3999. All rights reserved. Illustration by Thea Kliros.

## Chapter Nine
# The Great Escape

"Don't worry, Leon," Sprite said. "You'll turn back into a boy before that happens."

"Big deal," said Leon. "I'm sure that Meanie guy would put me in a zoo, anyway. As long as I'm in this pen, I'm in trouble."

Violet thought Leon had a good point. "We've got to get out of here," she said. "Then we can worry about tricking those dwarfs."

Sprite looked at his bound wings. "How are we supposed to do that?"

"We don't have much time," Violet said. "Leon, can you speak dog talk?"

"Of course. What do you think all that yipping was?" Leon asked.

"Good," Violet said. "I have an idea." She told Leon her plan.

Leon scratched behind his ear. "Sounds crazy. But I'll do it. I don't want to end up in a zoo!"

Leon turned to the dogs in the pen. *"Yip, yip, yip,"* Leon barked. *"Yip, yip, yip, yip!"*

The dogs all got quiet. Their ears perked up.

The biggest dog in the pen was a Saint Bernard. The dog walked over to the wall of the pen and stood still.

Then a hound dog jumped up on top of the Saint Bernard.

Buster, Brittany's beagle, climbed up on top of the hound dog.

Leon climbed up on top of Buster.

And finally, Sparky climbed on top of Leon.

"We did it," Leon called out. "What now?"

"You and Sparky should be able to jump over the top of the pen," Violet said.

Leon's nose twitched. "It's a long way down," he said.

"It's not that far," Violet said. "You can do it!"

Leon yipped something to Sparky. The little brown dog jumped out of the pen. Leon closed his eyes. Then he jumped, too.

"Wonderful!" Sprite said.

"Now come over here and chew through these leashes," Violet said.

Leon and Sparky bounded over to Violet and Sprite. They quickly freed Violet. Then Violet gently untied Sprite.

In the pen, the dogs barked loudly.

"I know," Violet said. "You want to be free, too."

Violet ran to the door of the pen and unlocked it. The dogs poured out, jumping and howling. They ran out of the clearing and into the woods.

"Will they be all right?" Sprite asked.

"They're going back to the dog park," Leon said.

"I'm sure their owners will find them there," Violet added.

Sprite sighed. "Then everything is going to be all right," he said.

Suddenly, a loud wail filled the clearing.

"My doggies!" Greenie cried. "The doggies are gone!"

Meanie stomped into the clearing behind his brother. "What have you done here? And who's that boy?"

Violet looked behind her. Leon had changed back into a boy. He was on his knees, scratching behind his ear.

Embarrassed, Leon stood up.

"Those dogs belong with their owners," Violet said. "It's wrong to take them to the Otherworld just so you can make money."

Greenie sniffed. "I don't care about money. I loved those doggies."

*"Yip! Yip!"*

"Leon, you can stop talking dog talk now," Sprite said.

"It wasn't me," Leon said. He pointed to Sparky.

Sparky hadn't run away with the other dogs. He barked and jumped into Greenie's arms.

Greenie hugged the little dog. "Do you want to stay with me?" he asked.

"But what about his owner?" asked Violet.

"I found Sparky all by himself," Greenie said. "He was all alone, poor little thing."

Sparky licked Greenie's face.

Violet had an idea. "Greenie, what if you could take Sparky back to the Otherworld with you?"

Greenie smiled. "Oh, yes! Oh, yes! I'll go home right now if you want me to."

Sprite understood what Violet had done. "You mean you'll do what we say? You'll obey us?"

Greenie nodded.

"Great!" Violet said. "You can get home through the oak tree in my backyard."

"Not so fast!" Meanie said.

The dwarf jumped in front of his brother. His eyes had turned an angry shade of red.

"My brother's not going anywhere without me," Meanie said. "And I'm not ready to go. Not without those dogs. I'm going to be rich! Rich!"

Sprite bravely flew in front of Meanie's face.

"You'll never do it," Sprite told him. "Not as long as we're around to stop you."

Meanie's eyes turned red. They started to glow.

"Then I'll put a spell on you," he said. "I'll make sure you and your friends don't cause me any more trouble!"

## Chapter Ten
# Beastie Bites

$V$iolet tried not to look into Meanie's eyes. She couldn't imagine what he was going to do. Turn them into stone? Make them disappear forever?

That's when she heard it.

*Crunch. Crunch. Crunch.*

Leon was munching on a handful of Beastie Bites cereal.

"Leon, how can you eat at a time like this?" asked Violet.

Leon shrugged. "Being a dog made me hungry. Mom put some in a bag for a snack this morning. It was in my pocket."

"Be quiet!" Meanie yelled. "You're ruining my spell!"

"Good!" Violet said. "You shouldn't put a spell on us, anyway! We're just trying to help."

"And I'm just trying to make some money," Meanie said. "Those dogs would have made me rich. There's nothing like them in the Otherworld."

Sprite's eyes lit up. He flew over to Leon. He took a piece of Beastie Bites cereal.

"There's nothing like this in the Otherworld, either," Sprite said. He handed the cereal to Meanie.

Meanie sniffed it. Then he popped it in his mouth.

Meanie didn't say anything at first. Then he broke into a big grin. His eyes stopped glowing.

"This stuff is great!" he said. He ran over to Leon and grabbed the bag.

"Hey!" Leon shouted.

"Let him have it, Leon," Violet said. "I think I know what Sprite is thinking. Right, Sprite?"

"Right," Sprite said. "Meanie, you can take

Beastie Bites back with you to the Otherworld. You can sell it there. The fairies will go crazy for it!"

Meanie stroked his beard. "You may be right. But I'd have to take back a lot."

"Not really," Sprite said. "One box should do. You can take it to the chefs in the Realm of Yum. They'll figure out how to make it for you. Then you can sell it and make lots of money."

"What's the Realm of Yum?" Leon asked.

"It's one of the lands in the Otherworld," Sprite explained. "You can get all kinds of wonderful food there. Except Beastie Bites, that is."

"Cousin Linguini is a chef in the Realm of Yum," Greenie pointed out. "He'll help us."

"This could work," Meanie said. "Where can I get a box?"

"At my house," Violet said quickly. "You can get back to the Otherworld from there, too."

"Then let's go!" Meanie said.

Sprite used pixie dust to take them all to Violet's backyard. Violet made Greenie and Meanie hide behind the oak tree. She didn't want Aunt Anne to see them.

Violet got a box of the cereal from her kitchen. She handed it to Meanie.

"There you go," she said. "Does this mean you will do what we say? You'll go back?"

"Sure," Meanie said. "These Beastie Bites are going to make me rich. Rich!"

Violet had to laugh. Meanie didn't look so scary now.

Greenie held Sparky tightly. "You'll like it in the Otherworld," he said. "I promise to take good care of you."

Violet looked around. Usually when a fairy was tricked, a wind tunnel came and took them away. But she was pretty sure the dwarfs had to go back on their own.

"This tree is a door to the Otherworld," she said.

"We know," said Meanie. "This is how we got here."

Meanie took a step into the tree. It was like the tree was made of air. He disappeared inside.

Greenie and Sparky followed.

"Tell the doggies I said good-bye!" Greenie called out behind him.

"Cool!" Leon said. Then he tried to disappear into the tree trunk, too. But he just banged his head.

"I guess it only works for dwarfs and fairies," Violet said.

## Chapter Eleven
# Don't Forget Finn

"See, Sprite," Violet said the next day. "We tricked them. Their pictures are here in the book."

Violet, Sprite, and Leon were eating breakfast in Violet's kitchen.

Since they were out of Beastie Bites, Violet's mom had made them a big plate of pancakes.

Leon licked the syrup from his plate.

"What would you guys do without me?"

Greenie and Meanie
love all dogs,
  They train them
in a special way.
  But to trick these
dwarf brothers,
You must get them
both to obey!

he asked. "You wouldn't be able to trick any pixies."

Violet sighed. Leon was such a show-off. But he deserved to brag a little. He hadn't complained at all about being turned into a dog.

Sprite hovered over a newspaper on the table.

"See here, Violet," he said. "There's more good news."

The article on the front page talked about how the missing dogs had all been found in the dog park.

"'It's a strange case,'" Violet read. "'No one seems to know where the dogs were. And owners have reported that their dogs can now do amazing tricks!'"

Violet laughed. "Greenie was a very good dog trainer," she said.

But Sprite didn't laugh. In fact, he looked very upset.

"Sprite, what's wrong?" Violet asked.

Sprite pointed to another headline on the page. It read, WIZ FINNSTER LEADS RACE FOR TOWN MAYOR.

"Oh, no!" Violet said. "I almost forgot.

# WIZ FINNSTER LEADS RACE FOR TOWN MAYOR

Election day is soon. If Finn wins, then he will be in charge of this town!"

"There's no telling what that evil wizard would do. We've got to do something right away!" Sprite said.

Leon frowned. "Can't we take a break?" he asked. "I'm still kind of tired from being turned into a dog and everything."

"If Finn becomes mayor, that would be worse than being a dog," Sprite said. "Worse than getting trapped inside a video game. Worse than having the hiccups. Worse than being turned into a fish-boy."

"Who got turned into a fish-boy?" Leon asked.

Violet held out her hand. "If we're going to stop him, we've got to work together. All for one. And one for all."

Sprite put his tiny hand on top of Violet's. "I'm in," he said.

Leon wiped his sticky hand on his jeans. "Me, too," he said.

"That settles it," Violet said. "We're going to stop Finn. We're going to save the human world. No matter what it takes!"

# Pixie Tricks Stickers

Place the stickers in the *Book of Tricks*.
You can find your very own copy of the *Book of Tricks*
in the first two books of the Pixie Tricks series,
*Sprite's Secret* and *The Greedy Gremlin*. When Sprite
and Violet catch a pixie, stick its sticker in the book.
Follow the directions in the *Book of Tricks* to complete
each pixie's page. (Pixie Secret: Some of these
pixies haven't been caught yet. Save
their stickers to use later.)